DATF

Nov. 1 | AG

A Bear
for Alice

A Bear
for Alice

story and pictures by
Lois Allen

Hawthorn Books, Inc.   Publishers   New York

For Ben, Amy, Joseph, and Peter

First Edition: 1970

"Joe," said Alice to her big brother, "I wish I had a bear for a pet. He would sit with me by the fire. It would be nice, wouldn't it?"

"No," Joe answered, "it would not be nice."

"I think it would be lovely," said Alice, beginning to look cross.

"Silly," Joe told her, "you can't trust a bear."

"Oh, I'd trust my bear," said Alice, frowning at Joe.

"If you read the newspapers once in a while," Joe said, "you would know that bears attack people all the time."

"My bear would not attack me," Alice whispered to herself.

A few days later on a sunny afternoon Alice went for a walk.
The long grass was blowing yellow, the sun was warm, and the earth
smelled sweet. Alice walked beneath the tall trees in the beech
woods not far from her house.

She sat awhile and leaned against the gray bark of a big
tree. The sun's rays filtered through the leaves and drew
changing yellow patterns on the green velvet moss. She thought
of her bear. Maybe he lived in this beautiful woods.

Just then Alice saw what looked like a bear, sunning himself
on the rocks not too far away. Very quietly, she went a little
closer. She curled up very small and looked. Yes, it was a bear.
His brown fur was shining red and gold in the sun. His nose was
brown, and he looked very big.

Alice sat still and listened. She could hear low grumbles. They sounded very lovely, not at all like the sounds a mean bear would make.

After a while the bear rose and stretched, and lumbered slowly away. Alice ran home to tell Joe that she had found her bear.

"There aren't any bears around here," Joe said. "Besides," he added, in a nagging big-brother way, "I told you to stay away from bears. They can't be trusted."

The next afternoon Alice went to the same woods, and there was her bear. She moved closer and closer. Then the big brown head turned and looked right at her. He had beautiful gray eyes as clear as the stream. There was hair on his face all the way to his nose. He had thick fur, and smelled very dark and warm. For a long time they sat there and looked at each other. Then the bear walked away. Slowly, Alice went home. She wondered how far her hand would go into the deep fur.

Alice ran home to tell Joe about her bear. She came running into the house, slamming the door behind her. "Joe," she shouted, "I saw the bear again today. I sat real close to him. How about that?"

Joe said, "Now don't go making up stories, Alice. There aren't any real bears around here."

"You may not believe me," said Alice, "but I saw a real bear just the same."

"Okay, okay," Joe answered. "If he is real you can take me to see him tomorrow."

Alice thought a minute, and said, "No, I won't take you tomorrow. He might run away if I bring you. Wait until he knows me better. Then I will introduce him to you."

"All right, I'll wait," said Joe, "but you had better not be kidding."

Every day Alice walked with her bear on the hills. They
wandered through sunburnt grass where grasshoppers buzzed, and
along the shady valley, with its clear water streaming around the
cool wet rocks. They strolled in the woods and rested in the sleepy
afternoon sun.

Alice called her bear Rug.

Rug and Alice were very happy. It seemed as if they had always been together.

When Rug stopped to fish in the stream, Alice waded in the pools. Sometimes she would swim in a deeper pool and dry off on a rock in the sun. She watched the minnows darting over the muddy bottom in the pockets between the rocks.

She followed the slow, sure movements of her bear. With a swift swing of a great wide paw, he would catch a shining, slippery fish.

Each day Alice told Joe everything that she and Rug had done. Joe wanted to see this bear friend that Alice talked about all the time, but Alice wouldn't take him with her to see him. She kept teasing him, saying, "Maybe one day soon. You'll just have to wait until Rug and I are ready for visitors."

What could Joe do but wait?

One day Rug began acting strange. He went through the grass so fast that Alice had to run to keep up with him. She stopped once to pick some wild bluebells, and he pushed her on roughly with his nose and growled. Alice became frightened. Maybe Joe was right. Maybe Rug could not be trusted. Finally Rug led her to a big hollow tree. They crawled inside and waited while Alice cried. She was really afraid.

All of a sudden the wind began to blow. The clouds darkened, and a storm began crashing all around them. Alice snuggled closer to Rug. "This is why he pushed me," she thought. "He knew the storm was coming, and he wanted to get us to a good dry place." The thunder boomed, the lightning lit the sky, and Alice, snug in a bear hug, smelled the delightful fragrances of summer rain, wood, and bear.

Leaves turned red and yellow, and fell to the ground. Acorns plopped and squirrels carried them in their fat cheeks to their nests.

One afternoon, Rug showed Alice his secret store of wild honey. He lifted her way up high. She dipped her fingers in and licked the honey. It was delicious.

She kept eating honey until she was sticky all over. When she told Joe about the wild honey, he begged her to take him with her. But Alice said, "No, not yet."

That night Joe made up his mind to follow Alice.

The very next day when Alice left the house, Joe was following her.

He did not know that Alice saw him out of the corner of her eye.

Alice did not go her usual way. She took Joe up the steepest hills and sloshed through muddy brooks. Alice got soaked but she didn't mind. Joe got soaked and he hated it.

Joe came home after Alice. He was pretty cross. "Funny thing," Alice said. "I didn't see Rug today. How come you're so wet?"

"I fell in a puddle," said Joe. "And why don't you quit talking about that bear, anyway? You're making the whole thing up," growled Joe.

"Someday I'll take you to see him, and then you'll see," said Alice smugly.

Then came one of the nicest days of all. Rug let Alice ride
on his back. He carried her all over the hills. She showed him her
house and told him all about Joe. He told her of the mountains
where he used to live, of the forests of slender white trees on
hills that rushed down to the crashing ocean's waves.

Summer was gone, a cold wind blew, and Alice, bundled up in a warm sweater, went out to find Rug. She looked in all of their favorite places, but he was nowhere. The woods were silent and empty.

"Maybe Rug has gone away," she thought. "Maybe I'll never see him again."

Alice looked and looked. At last she found Rug. He was asleep in his cave.

"Bears," he told her, "sleep all through the cold winter." But he would see her again in the spring, and they would have another wonderful summer.

It was a cold, lonely walk home.

"Joe," said Alice, sadly, "come now, and I'll show you Rug."
Joe did not believe Alice's bear was real, but he went with her
anyway.

They ran through the woods and over the fields. Alice led
the way through dry, crunchy leaves, blown into drifts by the wind.
There was the cave. Joe stood at the door. Alice crawled in.
She headed for the darkest corner. It was scary but Joe followed
her. Then, what do you think he saw?

ABOUT THE AUTHOR/ARTIST

Lois Allen attended the Art Academy and the University of Cincinnati.

She received two awards for her illustrations from the Art Director's Club of Cincinnati, and exhibited in a one-man art show in that city. Although she illustrated several children's books, A BEAR FOR ALICE was the first book she had written.

Mrs. Allen, who was also a second-grade teacher until her death in 1969, lived in Fort Mitchell, Kentucky, with her four children.